CHECKMATE IN SHADOWS

SHAILESH SINGH

Published by Shailesh, 2025.

"THE DARKEST TRUTHS ARE NOT HIDDEN
IN THE SHADOWS BUT ARE ETCHED INTO
THE LIGHT WE REFUSE TO SEE."

CONTENTS

Chapter 1: The First Cipher

Detective Aria Cole stood in the dimly lit living room, where the faint glow of streetlights seeped through torn curtains, casting eerie patterns on the walls. The scent of copper and decay hung thick in the air, mingling with the faint aroma of stale coffee from a forgotten mug on the side table. Her chest tightened as she surveyed the scene, a grim familiarity settling over her. Death always carried weight, no matter how many crime scenes she encountered.

The flickering light from a shattered lamp cast erratic shadows across the lifeless body sprawled on an ornate Persian rug. The victim, a middle-aged man, lay motionless, his vacant eyes fixed on the chandelier above. His face was frozen in an expression of shock, as though he had glimpsed his assailant at the very last moment.

Aria crouched beside the body, her gloved fingers hovering over an open book near the victim's outstretched hand. The book, an aged leather-bound volume titled *The Art of Cryptology*, bore scuffed edges and faint water stains that hinted at years of use. Its pages were yellowed, and faint pencil marks lined the margins, as if someone had studied it intently. It was opened to a dog-eared page, with the spine creased from repeated handling. Three numbers—12, 45, 78—were circled in bold red ink. The precision felt deliberate, each stroke calculated to grab attention.

"It's... eerie, isn't it?" Officer Liam Hayes' voice broke the silence. His normally confident tone faltered as he surveyed the unsettling scene. "Like he wanted us to find this."

Aria's sharp blue eyes scanned the surroundings. The cracked porcelain vase on the mantelpiece, the smudges on the coffee table, faint boot prints leading toward the door. Nothing felt random. Her gaze lingered on the circled numbers, the crimson ink contrasting starkly against the aged paper. A gnawing suspicion took root in her mind.

"They're not random," she replied, her voice steady. "They're a message. Or a clue."

As Aria reached for the book, something caught her eye—a faint imprint on the rug beneath the victim's hand. It looked like he had been clutching something tightly before his death. Whatever it was, it was gone now.

"Bag this book," she instructed Liam, handing it to him carefully. Liam hesitated for a moment, his brows furrowing as he studied the numbers on the page. "These numbers—what if they're more than pages?" he asked, his voice laced with unease. He glanced at Aria, searching her expression for reassurance, but her steely gaze remained fixed on the task at hand. "And dust the table and lamp for prints. Whoever did this left in a hurry."

A faint creak from the hallway made both officers turn sharply, weapons drawn. Aria held her breath, her ears straining to catch another sound. But the noise faded into silence, leaving only the distant hum of the streetlights outside.

"Get the evidence team in here," Aria said firmly, lowering her weapon. "We need to know what these numbers mean."

Liam nodded and stepped out to call for backup. Aria stayed crouched by the body, her mind racing. She flipped through the book again, careful not to disturb any evidence. The pages were filled with diagrams, codes, and handwritten notes in the margins. Some of the notes were in English, others in a language she didn't recognize. The circled numbers seemed to correspond to page numbers—pages that had been torn out.

"Deliberate," she murmured, tracing the jagged edge of a missing page. "This isn't just a message. It's a challenge."

The sound of camera flashes brought her back to the present. The evidence team had arrived, their movements precise and methodical. Aria stepped back to let them work, her thoughts still on the numbers.

"Detective," Liam's voice called from the hallway. "We've got something."

She followed him to the front door, where a small envelope had been tucked into the doorframe. The words "*For the detective*" were scrawled in neat, almost elegant handwriting. Aria tore the envelope open carefully, her pulse quickening. Inside was a single sheet of paper with a cryptic message:

"Every number holds a story. Every story hides a secret. Begin at 12."

Aria's mind raced as she read the note. Why "12"? She felt a gnawing unease, the kind that always came with the realization that she was being led into someone else's narrative. The phrase "Every number holds a story" resonated, reminding her of the circled numbers in the book. What stories did 12, 45, and 78 hold, and why were they significant enough to die for? Her grip tightened on the paper as a faint tremor of both dread and anticipation coursed through her.

She read the message aloud, her mind working furiously. "Page 12," she muttered. "But the page is missing from the book."

"Maybe the numbers aren't just pages," Liam suggested. "What if they're coordinates? Or a time?"

Aria nodded thoughtfully. She turned the paper over, looking for any additional clues. A faint watermark caught the light, revealing an emblem—a compass surrounded by intricate filigree. The design felt familiar, but she couldn't place it.

As she slipped the note into an evidence bag, a chilling thought crossed her mind. Whoever had left the note knew she would find it. And they knew she would take the bait.

For the first time in years, Aria felt a thrill of anticipation. This wasn't just a murder case. This was a game, and she had just made her first move.

That night, as Aria sat at her desk, she couldn't shake the feeling of being watched. The circled numbers haunted her thoughts. She opened her laptop and began searching for connections—to the book, the watermark, the numbers. Hours passed, and the pieces of the puzzle remained frustratingly out of reach.

Just as she was about to call it a night, her phone buzzed. It was a text from an unknown number:

"Check the clock."

Her eyes darted to the antique clock on her bookshelf, an heirloom passed down from her grandmother. Its ornate brass frame and delicately painted numbers spoke of a different era, a reminder of her childhood summers spent listening to her grandmother's stories of intrigue. The hands were at 12:45, a detail that sent a chill through her. Why had the killer chosen this specific time? Was it a mere coincidence, or did it hold a significance tied to the past she hadn't yet unraveled? A chill ran down her spine. The numbers weren't just random. They were everywhere, woven into the very fabric of the crime.

Aria grabbed her notepad and began jotting down every clue she had so far. The circled numbers, the missing pages, the cryptic note. The pieces were beginning to form a pattern, but the picture was still incomplete.

One thing was certain—the killer was toying with her. And Aria Cole wasn't one to back down from a challenge.

Chapter 2: Clues in the Library

The town library stood under the pale glow of the crescent moon, its stone façade weathered by countless seasons, exuding an air of silent authority. For most, libraries were sanctuaries of knowledge. But as Aria Cole stood at the heavy oak doors, clutching the cryptic note found at the crime scene, the building exuded a different aura—one of secrets and shadows.

Pushing the doors open, she stepped inside, the scent of aged paper and varnished wood wrapping around her like a shroud. The dim overhead lights cast flickering shadows, and the faint creak of the wooden floor echoed in the oppressive silence, amplifying the eerie atmosphere. Liam followed closely; his usual confident demeanor subdued by the quiet stillness. The rows of bookshelves stretched endlessly into the dimly lit interior; their shadows deepened by flickering overhead lights. It felt as though the library itself was alive, holding its breath.

Mrs. Eldridge, the elderly librarian, sat behind her desk, her pale blue eyes reflecting surprise and unease. Her silver hair, neatly pinned in a bun, trembled slightly as she adjusted her glasses, and her frail hands hovered over a worn ledger as though uncertain whether to close it or leave it open. She seemed more fragile tonight, her thin hands trembling slightly as she adjusted her cardigan.

"Detective Cole," she greeted, her voice a mere whisper. "You're here late. Is everything all right?"

Aria wasted no time. She held up the cryptology book from the crime scene, open to the page with the circled numbers. "Does this mean anything to you? The numbers—12, 45, 78—and this phrase: 'The truth hides where the shadows linger.'"

Mrs. Eldridge's expression darkened, her gaze darting toward the far end of the library. "Those numbers… they remind me of page markers. And that phrase—it sounds like something tied to our restricted collection. Follow me."

Without another word, the librarian led them deeper into the library. The air grew colder, and the faint hum of the lights above seemed to fade as they walked. When they reached a corner labelled 'Truths & Lies,' Mrs. Eldridge hesitated, her eyes scanning the shelves as if expecting something—or someone—to appear.

Aria stepped forward, her fingers trailing over the aged spines until they rested on a volume titled *Secrets of the Unseen*. Its cover was dark and worn, the title barely legible as though time itself sought to conceal its secrets. She pulled it free, and a folded piece of paper slipped from its pages, fluttering to the ground.

Unfolding it, Aria read aloud: "Begin where the clock stands still."

"Another clue," Liam muttered, stepping closer to examine the note. "But what clock?"

Aria's mind raced. She thought of the clock in the library's corner—an old fixture she'd seen during her last visit here, though she hadn't paid it much attention then. Could it be tied to the numbers?

"Mrs. Eldridge," Aria asked, turning back to the librarian, "the clock—does it still work?"

The librarian's face tightened. "No. It stopped years ago. The hands are frozen at 12:45."

The numbers struck Aria immediately. "12, 45… it's not just a time; it's part of the clue."

She approached the clock, its polished wooden frame gleaming faintly under the dim light. The carvings along its edges—stars and compasses—looked eerily familiar. Aria traced the patterns, her fingers brushing over an indentation at the base. A compartment popped open, revealing a small key and another slip of paper.

This time, the note read: "Unlock what the shadows guard."

"Mrs. Eldridge," Liam said, his tone sharp, "what's hidden in the restricted section?"

The librarian hesitated, then sighed heavily. "There's a collection of books locked away— texts too fragile or dangerous to leave out. But I don't know how this…" She gestured toward the key in Aria's hand. "…is connected."

Aria turned the key over, examining its intricate design. It was small but ornate, with a compass emblem engraved on its handle. The restricted section had to be their next destination.

"Show us the way," Aria said firmly.

Mrs. Eldridge led them to a locked cabinet at the back of the library. With trembling hands, she unlocked the glass doors, revealing a row of ancient, weathered tomes. One title immediately caught Aria's eye: *Shadows of the Mind.* It's dark cover bore the same compass symbol as the key.

Using the small key, she unlocked the book's clasp and opened it. Inside, the pages were filled with cryptic symbols and diagrams. At the very center, a folded map was tucked between the pages. Unfolding it, Aria saw coordinates and annotations scrawled in the same elegant handwriting as the previous notes. At the bottom, a chilling message read:

"You're closer, Detective. But the shadows deepen."

Liam peered over her shoulder. "Coordinates. Do you recognize them?"

Aria's stomach tightened as she traced the map's details. The marked location wasn't just familiar—it was deeply personal, tied to memories she'd rather keep buried. Her first major case had unraveled there, leaving scars she still carried. It was the abandoned clock tower at the edge of town—the same tower where her first major case had reached its bloody conclusion.

The killer wasn't just taunting her; they were tying the past and present into a dangerous game. And Aria knew the next move was hers.

Chapter 3: Shadows of the Victims

The records room hummed under the harsh glare of fluorescent lights, the stark brightness contrasting the dark undertones of their investigation. On the table before Aria, photographs of three victims lay side by side, their faces frozen in time. Each photograph was accompanied by an artifact left at the crime scenes: a worn book with numbers scrawled on its margins, a wooden carving of an ouroboros, and an antique pocket watch with the inscription, *Truth is found in reflection.*

Aria traced her fingers over the edge of the pocket watch, its smooth surface worn from time. "The killer is escalating," she said, her voice barely above a whisper. "These aren't just clues. They're pieces of a puzzle—no, a narrative. And they're leading us somewhere."

Liam stood on the other side of the table; his brows furrowed as he examined the ouroboros carving. "Why you?" he asked suddenly, looking up. "Why are they making this personal?"

Aria hesitated, her pulse quickening. She hadn't yet told him about the anonymous letter she'd received a week before the first victim was found. Its chilling words echoed in her mind: "*The shadows are watching you. And they remember*". The memory of that note burned in her thoughts, but revealing it now felt too dangerous, as though it might give the killer exactly what they wanted.

Instead, she deflected. "It's not about me. It's about the victims. There's something connecting them that we haven't uncovered yet."

She turned her attention to the crime scene photos. The first victim, a local historian, had been found in his study, surrounded by a sea of books. The second, a woodcarver, had been discovered in his workshop, a masterpiece left unfinished on his table. The third, a clockmaker, was found in his cluttered studio, gears and springs scattered like breadcrumbs.

Liam scrolled through his phone, cross-referencing their notes. "Books, carvings, clocks—these are deliberate choices. They're symbolic. But symbolic of what?"

Aria exhaled slowly, her eyes narrowing. "They're all creators," she murmured. "People who left behind legacies, tangible evidence of their existence. The killer isn't just choosing victims at random; they're targeting creators. But why?"

Her gaze fell to the inscription on the pocket watch again: *Truth is found in reflection.* The phrase tugged at her, its meaning just out of reach. Turning the watch over in her hand, she caught a glimpse of her own distorted reflection in its polished surface.

"Reflection," she said aloud, her mind racing. "What if it's not just literal? What if it's telling us to look deeper—into their lives, their work, their connections?"

Liam frowned. "You mean their creations might hold the next clue?"

"Exactly." Aria picked up the book from the first crime scene, its leather cover cracked with age. Flipping through its pages, she stopped when she reached the circled numbers from the margins—12, 45, and 78. Her mind flashed back to the clock in the library. Those numbers had led them to a map and a chilling message: *The shadows deepen.*

"This book," Aria said, her voice sharp. "It led us to the library. What if the killer is breadcrumbing us through their crimes, forcing us to uncover their pattern?"

Liam leaned closer, scanning the clues with fresh urgency. "If that's true, then the ouroboros carving and this pocket watch—"

"They're the next steps," Aria finished.

She picked up the carving, tracing its intricate details. The ouroboros, a serpent devouring its tail, was a symbol of cycles, eternity, and rebirth. Its design seemed oddly familiar, though she couldn't immediately place it.

"Wait," Liam said, his tone shifting. "There's something engraved on the back."

Aria flipped the carving over. Hidden within the grain of the wood was a faint inscription: *Where the past meets the present.*

Her breath hitched. "The clock tower," she whispered.

Liam nodded grimly. "The abandoned one. It's been standing there for over a century— watching the town's history unfold."

Aria felt her chest tighten. The clock tower had already been marked on the map they'd found in the library. Now, it was coming into focus as the centerpiece of the killer's twisted game.

"And this," she said, holding up the pocket watch, "might be the key to understanding what they're trying to tell us. We need to find out where it came from and who it belonged to."

The shadows in the room seemed to deepen as Aria stared at the artifacts, their meanings layered and elusive. The killer wasn't just taunting them; they were weaving a story—one that demanded Aria's full attention.

And somewhere within these cryptic clues, she knew the truth was waiting.

Chapter 4: Whispers in the Dark

Aria sat at her desk, the flickering glow of a desk lamp casting restless shadows across the room. The scattered clues before her felt like fragments of a language she hadn't yet learned to decode. Her eyes fell on the pocket watch from the third victim, its intricate design drawing her in once more. She turned it over, her fingers brushing the inscription: *Truth is found in reflection.*

The words had haunted her since the moment she read them, their meaning tantalizingly close yet maddeningly opaque. But tonight, she felt the answer was within reach.

She grabbed a small handheld mirror from her drawer, angling it against the watch's smooth surface. For a moment, nothing happened. Then, as she adjusted the angle, her breath caught. Letters emerged from the mirrored reflection, jagged and faint but unmistakable.

Nocturne Library, 10 PM.

Her heart raced. It wasn't just a clue—it was an invitation. Or worse, a trap.

Grabbing her phone, she dialed Liam, her voice steady but urgent. "Meet me at the library. Bring backup. This might be it."

Liam didn't argue. "On my way."

The Nocturne Library loomed ominously, its towering gothic architecture a stark silhouette against the velvety midnight sky. The faint hum of the city beyond was muffled here, as if the library existed in its own cocoon of eerie silence. Aria and Liam approached cautiously, their eyes scanning the darkened streets for any signs of movement. The notes clutched tightly in Aria's hands felt heavier with every step she took, as if it carried not just secrets but the weight of a malevolent past eager to resurface.

Chapter 5: An Unexpected Ally

The library doors groaned as they pushed them open, the sound reverberating through the cavernous interior. The grand reading hall stretched before them, its endless rows of bookshelves vanishing into shadows. Shafts of moonlight filtered through the stained-glass windows, casting fragmented, kaleidoscopic patterns across the polished floor. The air smelled of aged paper, dust, and something faintly metallic that set Aria's nerves on edge.

"Do you feel that?" Liam whispered, his hand instinctively resting on his holstered gun.

Aria nodded; her senses heightened. "Like we're being watched."

Before she could say more, a figure stepped out from the shadows, his movement fluid yet deliberate. He was a man of average build, dressed in a tweed jacket that gave him an air of harmless academia. But the glint in his eyes betrayed a depth of knowledge—and perhaps danger—that sent a chill down Aria's spine.

"Detective Aria Vega," the man said, his voice calm yet urgent. "I've been expecting you."

Aria's fingers tightened around her flashlight. "Who are you, and how do you know my name?"

The man raised his hands in a placating gesture. "Dr. Adrian Black. I've been researching the same web of corruption you've stumbled into. The killer's actions—what they're revealing—it's all connected. I can help you."

Liam stepped forward; his tone sharp. "Help us how? You've got about sixty seconds to convince us not to take you in for questioning."

Dr. Black's gaze shifted toward a nearby bookshelf, his demeanor unfazed. "There's something you need to see. Something that will make sense of the chaos."

Aria hesitated, trusting strangers in her line of work rarely ended well, but the urgency in Dr. Black's voice struck a chord. She gave Liam a subtle nod, signaling him to follow as Dr. Black led them deeper into the library.

They passed aisles of ancient tomes, their spines bearing titles in languages long forgotten. The library's oppressive silence was broken only by their footsteps, which seemed to echo endlessly in the vast space. At last, Dr. Black stopped in front of an ornate bookshelf, its wood intricately carved with swirling patterns.

"This shelf," he said, his fingers tracing the carvings, "is the key."

Aria raised an eyebrow. "To what?"

Without answering, Dr. Black pressed his fingers against a hidden panel. A faint groan echoed as the bookshelf shifted, revealing a hidden doorway. A blast of cold air rushed out, carrying with it the pungent scent of damp earth and mildew. The sound of a distant drip echoed from the darkened passage beyond.

"You're kidding me," Liam muttered, shining his flashlight into the yawning void. "A secret passage? What is this, a spy novel?"

Dr. Black ignored the comment, stepping into the passage. "Follow me. Time is of the essence."

The staircase beyond was narrow and steep, the stone steps slick with moisture. Aria gripped the cold stone wall for balance as they descended, the faint glow of their flashlights casting long, flickering shadows. The air grew colder the deeper they went, and the metallic tang that had been faint upstairs now became almost overpowering.

At the bottom of the stairs, they entered a cavernous chamber. The room was illuminated by the faint, otherworldly glow of symbols etched into the walls. The symbols pulsed faintly, as if alive, their glow casting eerie patterns across the room. In the center stood a large table covered in an assortment of maps, notebooks, and artifacts.

"This is where it all begins," Dr. Black said, gesturing to the table. "The killer's planning room."

Aria approached cautiously; her eyes drawn to a notebook emblazoned with the ouroboros symbol—the same symbol found on the victim's watch. Flipping through its pages, she found detailed sketches of crime scenes, cryptic diagrams, and notes referencing "Operation 78."

"What is this?" she murmured, holding up the notebook. Her heart skipped a beat as her eyes landed on a sketch of her childhood home, the number 78 scrawled prominently beneath it.

Dr. Black stepped closer, his expression grave. "Operation 78 was a classified initiative buried deep within the city's archives. Your father's name is directly tied to it, along with the names of the victims. The killer isn't just exposing corruption—they're dragging you into a nightmare woven from your own past."

Aria's grip on the notebook tightened, her breath quickening. Her father's cryptic warnings from her childhood now echoed in her mind, their significance finally clicking into place.

"This number—78," Liam said, examining the map pinned to the wall. "It keeps showing up. What does it mean?"

Dr. Black hesitated, his gaze flickering toward Aria. "It's not just a number. It's a code—a key to unlocking the truth. And the truth… is far darker than you can imagine."

Dr. Black pulled a leather-bound journal from the desk and handed it to her. "Your family's past is intricately tied to this case. The killer is forcing you to confront it. They've chosen you for a reason."

Aria's fingers trembled as she opened the journal. The pages were filled with detailed sketches, newspaper clippings, and handwritten notes. The ouroboros symbol appeared repeatedly, alongside cryptic phrases like *What lies beneath will rise again* and *The sins of the father are never forgotten.*

Her heart sank as she came across a diagram linking her father's name to a decades-old corruption scandal—one that had been buried under layers of deceit. It wasn't just a case; it was a reckoning.

Liam leaned over her shoulder; his expression dark. "This is insane. Why didn't we know about this?"

"Because it was meant to stay hidden," Dr. Black said, his tone grim. "The killer is unraveling secrets that were buried long ago. And they're using you to expose them, Detective."

A sudden noise shattered the tense silence. The sound of hurried footsteps echoed from the passageway behind them. Aria and Liam spun around; their weapons drawn.

"Someone's here," Liam said.

They bolted back up the staircase, their flashlights bouncing wildly with their movements. By the time they reached the library's main hall, the doors were ajar, swinging gently in the breeze. Whoever had been spying on them was gone.

Aria stared into the empty street beyond, her mind racing. The shadows seemed to close in around her, whispering secrets she wasn't sure she wanted to hear.

"Liam," she said, her voice steady despite the turmoil within. "We're not just chasing a killer anymore. We're chasing the truth. And we're running out of time."

Chapter 6: Secrets in the Shadows

The revelations from the hidden chamber lingered in Aria's mind like a storm cloud. Back at the precinct, the atmosphere was heavy with the weight of their discovery. Aria, Liam, and Dr. Black gathered around the evidence table, where the journal, maps, and artifacts from the library's secret chamber were spread out in stark detail. Each item seemed to pulse with unspoken truths, demanding to be unraveled.

"Operation 78," Aria began, her tone sharp and deliberate. "It keeps coming up. The killer's actions, the journal, even the symbols in the tunnels—everything points back to it. And now my father's connection. This can't be a coincidence."

Dr. Black leaned forward; his expression shadowed by worry. "Operation 78 was a covert city project-initiated decades ago. Officially, it was presented as an ambitious urban renewal program aimed at revitalizing the city's most neglected areas. But unofficially…" he hesitated, glancing at Aria. "Unofficially, it became a breeding ground for corruption. There were whispers of illegal land deals, extortion, and even the disappearances of those who opposed it. Your father, Detective Aria, was one of its chief architects."

Aria's chest tightened at his words. The memories of her father's long nights at his desk, the hushed phone calls, and his cryptic warnings began to surface. He had always spoken of building a legacy, but never in terms that hinted at anything sinister. "He… he was a good man," she said, her voice trembling slightly. "Whatever mistakes he made; he didn't deserve this."

Liam, always the pragmatist, tapped the large map pinned to the wall. Red strings connected various locations, some marked with 'X' while others remained untouched. "If this is the killer's blueprint, they've been precise. Every site they've hit ties back to Operation 78. But look at these—locations they haven't targeted yet. Are they future targets? Or are they hiding something even bigger?"

Dr. Black moved closer to the map, his finger tracing the lines until it stopped at an abandoned courthouse in the city's oldest district. "This site hasn't been touched yet, but historically, it was central to the project's inception. If there's any evidence left, it would be here."

The courthouse loomed before them, a decaying relic of a bygone era. Its weathered facade bore the scars of time, and vines crept over its once-grand columns like skeletal fingers. Broken windows stared out like hollow eyes, and the air was thick with the scent of mildew and decay. The team approached cautiously, their flashlights piercing the oppressive darkness inside.

The interior was a stark reminder of its abandonment. Dust blanketed every surface, and the faint scurrying of rats echoed through the desolate halls. In the main chamber, they found another chilling display: a pedestal surrounded by scattered photographs, documents, and a single envelope marked "Aria."

Aria's hands trembled as she opened the envelope. Inside was a letter, its words scrawled in jagged handwriting:

Detective Aria,

"The truth lies buried where it began. You know the number. Find it before it finds you."

Enclosed was a torn page from an old city ledger. The imprint of "78" was faint but unmistakable. Aria flipped it over, revealing a faded blueprint of an underground tunnel system beneath the city. Her heart pounded as the implications sank in.

Dr. Black examined the page closely. "These tunnels were part of Operation 78's original design. They connected key sites across the city—backdoors, escape routes, hidden vaults. If the killer has been using them, it explains how they've managed to stay ahead of us."

Liam's jaw tightened. "We need to find these tunnels. They could lead us straight to the killer."

Suddenly, a metallic clang echoed from the far end of the chamber, followed by hurried footsteps. Aria signaled for silence; her weapon drawn. The team moved in unison, advancing cautiously toward the source of the noise.

At the back of the chamber, they discovered a hidden trapdoor, its edges worn from use. Aria descended first, her flashlight cutting through the dense darkness. The air grew colder with every step, carrying the faint scent of damp earth and rust. The tunnel walls were lined with faintly glowing symbols—the same ones they had seen in the library's hidden chamber.

At the tunnel's end, they entered a small, dimly lit room. A single bulb hung from the ceiling, casting flickering shadows across the walls. The centerpiece of the room was a mural—a vivid depiction of the ouroboros encircling the city skyline. Beneath it, a phrase was etched in blood-red paint: *"What was hidden shall be revealed."*

Aria's eyes locked on the mural, her pulse quickening. The symbols, the tunnels, her father's involvement—all of it pointed to one undeniable truth. The killer's actions weren't just about exposing corruption. They were personal.

"This isn't just about the city," Liam said, his voice tight. "It's about you."

Aria's resolve hardened. She turned to her team, her eyes blazing with determination. "We're not done yet. The killer's been playing a game, but now we have the pieces to fight back. And when we find them, this ends—once and for all."

Chapter 7: Shadows of the Asylum

The next morning brought no clarity, only more questions. Aria sat in her office; the contents of the journal spread across her desk. Each page was a labyrinth of cryptic statements, coded symbols, and unsettling sketches. The ouroboros appeared repeatedly, always accompanied by variations of the same phrase: *"When the serpent consumes its tail, the cycle will end."*

A knock at the door interrupted her thoughts. Adrian entered, holding a stack of old files. "I dug these up from the archives," he said. "Records from Elderidge Asylum. Most of them are redacted, but there's enough here to connect your father to their operations."

Aria sifted through the files, her chest tightening with every page. Her father's name appeared frequently, always linked to something called *Operation 78.* The more she read, the clearer it became that the asylum hadn't been a sanctuary for the mentally ill—it had been a front for something far darker.

"They were conducting experiments," Aria murmured, her voice thick with disgust. "Using patients as test subjects to... what? Advance their agenda?"

Adrian hesitated before responding. "To create leverage. Elderidge was a testing ground, but also a place where the organization stored its most sensitive secrets. If the killer wants you to go there, it's because they believe those secrets will expose everything."

Liam joined them, a determined look on his face. "Then we go. But we go prepared."

Elderidge Asylum loomed like a specter on the horizon, its silhouette jagged and crumbling against the stormy sky. The building was a monument to decay, its once-grand facade now a mosaic of shattered windows and creeping ivy. The air around it felt colder, as if the very ground rejected their presence.

"This place is cursed," Liam muttered, gripping his flashlight tightly.

Aria ignored the comment, her focus on the asylum's rusted gates. They creaked ominously as she pushed them open, the sound echoing through the empty grounds. "Stay close," she instructed. "We don't know what we're walking into."

The main hall was a cavernous expanse of shadows and dust. Broken furniture and scattered papers littered the floor, and faint graffiti covered the peeling walls. Symbols similar to those in the journal adorned several surfaces, their crimson paint stark against the gray backdrop.

"Over here," Adrian called, his flashlight illuminating a staircase leading downward. "The records room should be below."

The basement was colder, the air damp and heavy with mildew. They found the records room at the end of a narrow corridor, its steel door ajar. Inside, filing cabinets lined the walls, their drawers spilling yellowed documents onto the floor.

Aria's eyes immediately fell on a file marked with her father's name. She opened it with trembling hands, her breath catching as she read the contents. The document detailed *Operation 78,* a classified project involving psychological manipulation and forced compliance. Her father's role was listed as *Lead Consultant.*

"This can't be true," Aria whispered, her voice breaking. "He wasn't like this."

Adrian placed a reassuring hand on her shoulder. "Aria, whatever he was involved in, it doesn't define who he was to you. But this... this is part of the truth the killer wants us to see."

A sudden sound—a faint whisper—made them freeze. The whisper grew louder, morphing into an unintelligible cacophony that seemed to emanate from the walls themselves.

"We're not alone," Liam said, his voice tense.

The whispers led them to another room deeper in the basement. Inside, they found a shrine-like setup. The ouroboros symbol dominated the far wall, painted in bold strokes of crimson. Beneath it, an altar held artifacts tied to Aria's family: photographs, trinkets, and a recorder with a note attached: *"Play me."*

Aria pressed play, and a distorted voice filled the room.

"Detective Aria Bennett. You stand on the precipice of truth. Your family's sins are etched into this city's foundation. I am not your enemy—I am the reckoning. The cycle ends with you."

The recording ended abruptly, leaving a chilling silence. Aria stared at the recorder, her heart pounding. "They're trying to make this personal," she said. "To make me question everything I know."

A hidden mechanism clicked. The door slammed shut, and the room filled with a hissing sound.

"Gas!" Adrian shouted, pulling his shirt over his face.

Aria's vision blurred as the room filled with thick mist. She stumbled toward the door, but her strength was fading. Just before she lost consciousness, she saw a shadowy figure step into the room.

"Not yet, Detective," the figure said. "The truth must be earned."

When Aria awoke, she was lying outside the asylum, the rain soaking her clothes. Liam and Adrian were beside her, groaning as they stirred. She sat up, her head pounding. A slip of paper was tucked into her jacket pocket. It read: *"The serpent devours itself, but the cycle remains unbroken. Are you ready to see it through?"*

Aria clenched the note in her fist, her resolve hardening. The killer wanted her to play their game. Fine. But she would play by her own rules—and she wouldn't stop until she unearthed every shadow, every lie.

As she stood, her eyes turned back to the asylum. Its decaying walls seemed to watch her, a silent witness to the horrors within. She had stepped into the killer's world, but she wasn't alone—and she wasn't afraid.

"This isn't over," she said aloud, her voice steady. "Not by a long shot."

Chapter 8: Echoes of the Asylum

The sun dipped below the horizon as Elderidge Asylum came into view, its decayed silhouette outlined against the indigo sky. The building loomed like a tombstone for forgotten lives, its barred windows and ivy-covered walls whispering secrets of its dark past.

"This place doesn't just look haunted—it feels haunted," Liam muttered, his unease evident as he scanned the grounds. His hand lingered on his holstered gun, a silent acknowledgment of the danger they were walking into.

Adrian adjusted the strap of his backpack, his tone clipped. "Haunted or not, this place holds answers. We need to stay sharp—whoever's been playing us might still be here."

Aria remained silent, her focus on the imposing structure ahead. Every step toward the asylum felt heavier, the weight of her father's secrets pressing down on her. She tightened her grip on her flashlight, its cold metal grounding her in the moment.

The asylum's front doors groaned in protest as Adrian pushed them open, revealing the familiar yet no less unnerving interior. The air was damp and stale, carrying a faint metallic tang that sent a chill down her spine.

Inside, the asylum seemed even more derelict than before. Warped floorboards creaked under their boots, and the once-faded murals lining the walls now seemed grotesque under the flickering beams of their flashlights. Graffiti scrawled in red paint covered every surface—symbols, arrows, and cryptic phrases like *"The serpent awakens"* and *"Roots in blood."*

"This place feels... different," Liam whispered, his voice barely audible.

"They've been here again," Aria said, gesturing toward a fresh trail of markings on the walls.

"This is deliberate. They're leading us somewhere."

The group moved cautiously, their flashlights casting long shadows that seemed to twist and writhe along the walls. Every sound—every creak, every distant rustle—set their nerves on edge.

As they approached the central hall, Aria's flashlight landed on a rusted wheelchair lying on its side. Nearby, an overturned file cabinet spilled yellowed records across the floor. Aria knelt, picking up one of the files.

It listed the name of a patient admitted for "delusional paranoia." The details were chillingly familiar—the admission dates overlapped with the years her father had been tied to the asylum. Scribbled in the margins was a note: *"Operation 78: Witness secured."*

Adrian leaned over her shoulder. "Operation 78? That's not a coincidence."

"It's not," Aria replied, her voice tight. "Whatever this is, it started long before we got involved."

They followed the red markings to the central hall. The cavernous space was dominated by the massive mural of an ouroboros, its eternal cycle etched in cracked and peeling paint. Beneath it, a desk stood as though waiting for them, its surface cluttered with files, a weathered journal, and a tape recorder.

Aria hesitated before pressing play.

The recorder hissed to life, static crackling before a distorted voice began to speak:

"The truth lies beneath the surface, Detective. Every secret has its roots, and every root is nourished by blood. You've come far, but you've only scratched the surface. Will you dare to dig deeper?"

The recording cut off abruptly, leaving an oppressive silence.

"What the hell does that mean?" Liam asked, his voice low.

"They're taunting us," Adrian said, his gaze shifting to a partially concealed trapdoor in the corner. "But I think they also want us to find something."

The trapdoor resisted at first, its hinges rusted and groaning, but Aria managed to pry it open. A set of stone stairs descended into darkness, the air colder and more oppressive with each step.

"This is where it gets worse," Liam muttered, gripping his flashlight like a lifeline.

The stairs led to an underground chamber. The sight that greeted them was grotesque: shelves lined the walls, filled with jars containing preserved specimens—organs, bones, even what appeared to be severed fingers. The dim light from a surgical lamp above cast eerie shadows across the room.

In the center stood a steel table, its surface scarred and stained. Aria's breath hitched when her flashlight illuminated the stack of photographs resting atop it.

The faces staring back at her were her family. The photographs spanned decades, showing candid moments that were never meant to be seen by strangers. Each one was marked with dates and cryptic notes—observations, coordinates, and phrases like *"Stage one complete"* and *"Unveiling imminent."*

"They've been watching you," Adrian said grimly, his voice low.

Liam picked up a recent photograph of Aria standing at the last crime scene. Beneath it was a note scrawled in jagged handwriting: *"You're almost ready."*

"This isn't just obsession," Aria whispered, her hands trembling. "This is... ritualistic."

As the group processed the chilling discovery, a faint, rhythmic thumping sound echoed from a door at the far end of the room. The noise was almost imperceptible, like the heartbeat of the asylum itself.

Adrian raised his flashlight toward the door, his jaw tightening. "That can't be good."

Aria nodded, her pulse quickening. "But we have to see what's there."

The door led to a smaller room, its walls covered in more symbols and writings. In the center stood a pedestal, and atop it lay a journal. Aria approached cautiously, her eyes scanning the surroundings for any signs of a trap.

The journal's cover was cracked leather, its pages yellowed with age. She flipped it open, her breath catching as she read the erratic scrawl within.

One passage stood out: *"The serpent's cycle feeds on the blood of its roots. The detective holds the key, but the final act requires her to see beyond the veil."*

"What does that even mean?" Liam asked, frustration creeping into his voice.

"It means they're pulling me into their delusion," Aria said, her voice shaking. "But this... this isn't just a game to them. It's a ritual. A cycle they think I'm meant to complete."

Before they could analyses further, a loud crash reverberated from the floors above. Heavy footsteps followed, deliberate and menacing.

"They know we're here," Adrian said, his voice tense.

"Or they planned for us to be," Aria added, gripping the journal tightly.

"Either way, we're leaving now," Liam said, motioning toward the trapdoor.

The team moved quickly, retracing their steps. The asylum seemed to come alive around them—the walls whispered unintelligibly, and shadows danced in the corners of their vision. The cacophony of sounds grew louder, almost overwhelming, as they reached the exit.

Outside, the cold night air wrapped around them like a protective shield, but the unease remained. Aria turned back, the asylum's dark windows staring back at her like soulless eyes.

"They wanted us to find this journal," she said, clutching it tightly. "But this isn't over. They're pushing me toward something bigger. Something I don't fully understand yet."

Liam frowned. "And what if it's a trap?"

"It probably is," Aria admitted, her gaze hardening. "But it's the only lead we have—and I'm not stopping now."

Chapter 9: The Game Unfolds

The asylum stood like a sentinel of despair behind them as Aria, Liam, and Adrian exited its shadowed confines. The chill in the air did little to numb the whirlwind of emotions raging within each of them. The discovery inside—the cryptic photographs, the chilling recordings, the relentless recurrence of symbols—had confirmed their fears.

This wasn't just about a deranged killer. This was personal. The killer had chosen Aria as the centerpiece of a macabre game, a twisted narrative where she was both the protagonist and the prey.

The drive back to the precinct was somber, words scarce but the tension palpable. Aria sat in the back seat, her fingers absently tracing the edge of the leather-bound journal they had retrieved. Her mind churned through memories of her father, the fragments of his work, and the terrifying truth that was beginning to surface.

When they reached the precinct, they immediately made their way to the briefing room. The normally bustling atmosphere of the station felt distant, muted. The room, dimly lit by a single fluorescent light overhead, became their war room. The table, now cluttered with photographs, recordings, maps, and documents, seemed to mirror the chaos of their investigation.

Aria stood at the table's edge, staring down at the scattered pieces of the puzzle. Her voice broke the silence.

"This is all about my father," she said firmly. "His work at the asylum, the experiments, the organization—it's all connected. And now, they've dragged me into it."

Adrian, standing to her right, set down another stack of documents he'd been combing through since they left the asylum. His expression was grim. "Your father wasn't just a doctor at the asylum, Aria. He was deeply involved in a covert operation—something called 'Project Fear Reclamation.' It was meant to explore ways of using fear therapeutically, but it turned into something darker."

Liam leaned against the wall, arms crossed, his skeptical tone cutting through the tension. "Darker how?"

Adrian glanced at him. "They weren't just treating fear; they were trying to harness it, weaponize it. They believed that fear could be manipulated to control behavior, even break minds. Your father was a key figure in the project, but from what I've read, he eventually tried to stop it. That's when things went sideways."

"Sideways how?" Aria asked, her voice tight.

Adrian hesitated. "He tried to expose what they were doing. He filed reports, contacted outside authorities. But the organization buried him. His reputation was destroyed, and any evidence he had vanished with him."

Aria clenched her fists, her knuckles white against her skin. "And now this killer is using my father's work to justify their own atrocities. It's like they're carrying on his legacy but twisting it into something monstrous."

Her eyes moved to the map pinned to the wall. The asylum was marked at its center, with red strings connecting it to other locations. Her childhood home was one of them, but several others remained unexplored. Each string felt like a tether pulling her closer to the killer's endgame.

"These locations," she murmured, tracing the strings with her finger. "What do they mean? If the killer's plan is as meticulous as it seems, these places aren't random."

Liam stepped forward, holding the journal they had retrieved from the hidden chamber. "This manifesto—it's more than just a diary. It's a guide. Every murder, every clue, every move they've made—it's all here."

He flipped through the pages, stopping at a list of dates written in jagged handwriting. Each one was accompanied by brief notes, cryptic phrases that matched details from the previous murders.

"Look at this," Liam said, pointing to the final entry. "Three days from now. 'The queen's sacrifice completes the game.'"

Aria's blood ran cold. "The queen..."

Her voice faltered, but Liam finished her thought. "It's you. They're planning to kill you."

The room fell silent, the weight of his words pressing down on them like a physical force. Adrian broke the stillness, his voice calm but resolute. "Then we don't give them the chance. If they want you to play their game, we'll make sure we're the ones setting the rules."

Aria nodded, her resolve hardening. "We need to figure out their next move. If we can decode these clues, we'll know where to strike first."

Adrian turned his attention to the numbers that had appeared repeatedly in their investigation—*12* and *45*. They had dismissed them initially as coincidental, but the pattern was too consistent to ignore.

"These numbers—they're not random," Adrian said. "The first victim's watch stopped at 12:45. The second victim's clock was shattered at the same time. At the asylum, the same numbers were scrawled on the walls. The killer is trying to tell us something."

"Or taunting us," Liam added.

Aria's mind raced, pulling at threads of memory. "Twelve and forty-five—they're a time, yes, but maybe they're more than that. What if they're a pattern, a countdown, or a coordinate?"

Adrian's brow furrowed. "A coordinate? That could tie to the locations on the map."

Aria nodded. "It's worth exploring. And we need to figure out what happens at that exact time. If they're planning their next move at 12:45, we have less time than we thought."

The trio split the tasks between them. Adrian began cross-referencing the map locations with the journal's entries, while Liam started combing through surveillance footage and timelines for patterns. Aria stayed behind in the briefing room, poring over the journal and photographs.

As the hours ticked by, she felt the pieces of the puzzle begin to shift into place, though the picture they formed was still incomplete. The killer wasn't just after her—they were orchestrating a finale, a grand performance with her at its center. But Aria vowed that she wouldn't play the role they had written for her.

The numbers *12* and *45* loomed in her mind, like the ticking of a clock counting down to an inevitable confrontation. But she refused to let fear dictate her next move. If the killer wanted a game, then she would rewrite the rules—and make sure that she was the one holding the checkmate.

After several attempts Aria leaned over the map, her fingers tracing the jagged edges of the highlighted coordinates. Something about the name "Shadow Creek" sent a shiver down her spine.

"This place…" she murmured, the memory faint but persistent. "I've heard of it before. My father mentioned it once, but he never told me why. He just said it wasn't safe."

Liam raised an eyebrow. "Not safe? Like, dangerous people or something more… hidden?"

"I don't know," Aria admitted, shaking her head. "But it was enough to scare him. And my father wasn't afraid of much."

Adrian tapped the journal, his tone thoughtful. "Shadow Creek shows up here more than once, usually paired with dates and times. It could be where they're planning their next move—or where it all started."

Aria's unease grew as she stared at the map, the name "Shadow Creek" practically taunting her. "If it's where they want us to go, then we don't have a choice. But something tells me we're walking straight into a trap."

Chapter 10: The Reckoning at Shadow Creek

Shadow Creek was never just a name—a ghost from Aria's childhood, a place her father had taken her to once, years before his downfall. Nestled in the shadows of misty hills, the town's name had surfaced repeatedly in Adrian's cross-referencing of the journal and map. It wasn't just the next move; it felt like the killer's endgame. With "12:45" etched in their minds, the trio followed the trail, aware that this might be a trap.

The journey to Shadow Creek was heavy with silence. Aria sat clutching the journal, its cryptic markings their only guide. Memories tugged at the edges of her mind—her father's nervous glances, his hushed warnings during their last visit to the town. What had he been hiding? The streets of Shadow Creek were eerily deserted, their silence a stark contrast to its once-bustling charm. Boarded windows and cracked asphalt whispered of decay. The coordinates led them to "Creekside Industrial," a rusted factory that loomed like a ghost from another era. Its gates hung askew, bearing the scars of neglect.

"This place feels like a graveyard," Liam muttered, cutting the engine.

Aria's gaze lingered on the structure. "My father knew this place. He brought me here, but he wouldn't say why. I think he was afraid of it."

Adrian checked his watch. "We have fifteen minutes."

The trio ventured inside, the air thick with the scent of rust and mildew. Their footsteps echoed in the vast, hollow space. The journal's final pages described this place in chilling detail—a labyrinth of forgotten machinery and a central room where "the queen's sacrifice" would unfold.

Massive wooden chess pieces stood as sentinels, scattered throughout the corridors, their bases inscribed with the symbols they had seen in the journal. "The Queen's Gambit,"

"Sacrifice for victory," and "Checkmate is inevitable" were scrawled across the walls in a macabre script.

The central chamber was illuminated by a spotlight, revealing a massive chessboard etched into the floor. At its centre, a figure sat slumped in a chair—bound and gagged. Aria's breath caught as she recognized the curator of the asylum: Evelyn Harper.

Adrian and Liam rushed forward, but a distorted voice crackled through the factory's speakers. "Welcome, Aria," it boomed. "You've played the game well. But the final move is yours."

Evelyn, began to thrash, her muffled screams filling the room. Adrian removed her gag, and she gasped, "I didn't want this... They forced me."

"What do you mean?" Aria demanded, her eyes narrowing.

Evelyn's voice broke with desperation. "They're everywhere. Your father tried to stop them, but they made an example of him. They made me their pawn."

The killer's voice interrupted. "Ah, Evelyn, always the journalist turned captive queen. Tell them, Aria, how your father played this game and lost."

A panel slid open, revealing a glass-walled room filled with monitors. Inside stood a masked figure—the Architect.

"You want to know why, Aria?" the Architect sneered. "Because you are your father's legacy. His defiance set this in motion. You are the queen, the key to finishing the game."

The spotlight shifted to a countdown timer on the wall: 12:43. The Architect gestured toward the chessboard. Two pawns—one black, one white—were missing.

"This is your move, Aria. Choose wisely, and you might survive."

Aria's mind raced. Every clue in the journal, every move in this twisted game, had led to this moment. The numbers weren't just a time—they were coordinates on the board.

"Adrian, move the queen to twelve-forty-five!" she yelled.

Adrian complied, sliding the white queen into place. The timer halted at 00:01. For a moment, silence reigned. Then the Architect's voice filled the room once more.

"Well played, Aria. But the game has only begun."

Smoke flooded the chamber, and when it cleared, the Architect was gone. Evelyn clung to Aria, trembling.

"You're coming with us," Aria said, her voice like steel. "No more secrets."

As they stepped into the cold night, the factory loomed behind them—a haunting reminder of the Architect's reach. Aria vowed to end the game, not as a pawn, but as a player in control.

EPILOGUE

Snow blanketed shadow creek as aria stared into the quiet streets. Evelyn harper, once a fearless investigative journalist, had revealed the truth: she had worked with aria's father to expose a clandestine organization orchestrating crimes through elaborate games. But when they delved too deep, the organization turned on them. Evelyn had been forced to follow the Architects plan and whatever he says and made forced into silence; her family threatened.

Back at the car, Adrian and Liam waited, their exhaustion evident. The journal lay in aria's lap—a stark reminder of how close they had come to losing.

"This isn't over," she said. "The architect is still out there."

Adrian nodded. "Next time, we'll be ready."

As the car disappeared into the night, aria clutched the journal. The chessboard lingered in her mind, a symbol of the architect's shadowy empire. The queen had survived, but the king remained hidden. And aria knew their next encounter would determine the final checkmate.